¡An Oinkrrific Day!

A Musical, Bully-Busting,
Barnyard Adventure

By Jean Voice Dart
Illustrated by Anastasia Yatsunenko

An Oinkrrific Day!
A Musical, Bully-Busting, Barnyard Adventure

Copyright © 2021 by Jean Voice Dart.
All rights reserved.
Printed in the USA

www.jeanvoicedart.com

This is just a fancy way of saying please be honest and kind.
Don't copy the pages or try to get credit for something that you didn't create yourself.
Instead, go to our website for lots of fun, free stuff at www.jeanvoicedart.com. Thank you.

A portion of book proceeds is donated
to registered children's charities. Thank you.

Library of Congress Control Number: 2019912996
Available in hardcover, softcover, e-book, and audiobook.
Paperback: 978-1-64085-899-2
Hardback: 978-1-64085-900-5
Ebook: 978-1-64085-901-2

Published by Author Academy Elite
P.O. Box 43, Powell, OH 43065
www.AuthorAcademyElite.com

To my mother, who lovingly whistled and
sang to us from the comfort of our big, green, rocking chair.
And most importantly, with heartfelt love and encouragement
to everyone searching for their unique heart song.

I believe in you!

On a farm far away,
In a house made of hay, . . .

. . . Lived nine pigs and a runt,
Who sat down with a grunt.
He said, "Oink, oink, hooray!
It's an *oinkrrific* day!"

"It's an oinkity, oinkity, Oinkrrific day!"

Piggies knew what to do.
Snorty hid. Lilac drew.
Piggies all in one room.
Hammy said, "Zoom, zoom, zoom!"
Piggies here. Piggies there.
Bitsy in a green chair.

Squeaker played peekaboo.
Blossom wore her tutu.
Scrappy knelt on the rug.
Bernie felt a warm hug.
Snappy's blocks stood so tall.
Mama sang to them all.

Bernie said, "Help me sing.
It's the *oinky* best thing."

Mama said, "Trust your heart.
It's the best place to start."

"Don't be me. Just be you.
Find the sound that is true!"

Bernie said, "I will try!"
And he gave a deep sigh.

Bernie squawked when he tried.
They said, "Stop. Go outside!
You sound bad. Do not sing.
It's the *oinky* worst thing!"

Bernie said, "You are wrong.
I will write a new song.
The right sound will be found.
I'll search house, sky, and ground!"

So they yelled and they frowned.
"No, your sound can't be found!"

"You are *oinkity* wrong.
You cannot write a song!"

"You must leave. Run away.
Leave our house made of hay!"

"Go away. Go outside.
Leave this house. Run and hide!"

Bernie cried. He was sad.
And that night he was mad.
He said, "I don't feel glad.
I feel *oinkity* bad."

He was first sad and mad.
Then he felt brave and glad!
He said, "No, they are wrong!
I will write the best song!

"It's a sound just for me.
It's the best symphony.
It's my sound. Yessirree!
It's my own *pigphony*.

"Yes, my sound will be found.
It will be the best sound.
It's an *oinkity, oinkrrific,*
Pigphony sound!"

Then he met Cassie Lou,
Who said, "Hi, how are you?
It's a cawrrific day.
Caw, caw, caw. Hip hooray!"

Bernie asked, "Can you play?
Can you help me today?
Can you please find my sound?
I searched house, sky, and ground!"

Then he met Cluckydoo
Who said, "Hi, how are you?
It's a *cluckrrific* day.
Cluck, cluck, cluck. Hip hooray!"

Bernie asked, "Can you play?
Can you help me today?
Can you please find my sound?
I searched house, sky, and ground!"

"Yes, I can! Yessiree!
You'll make music with me.
It's a *cluckrrific* sound.
It's the best sound around!"

"That's a wonderful sound!
But my sound must be found.
It's been nice meeting you.
Toodle-oo, Cluckydoo!"

Then he met Daisy Sue,
Who said, "Hi, how are you?
It's a cheeprrific day.
Cheep, cheep, cheep. Hip hooray!"

Bernie asked, "Can you play?
Can you help me today?
Can you please find my sound?
I searched house, sky, and ground!"

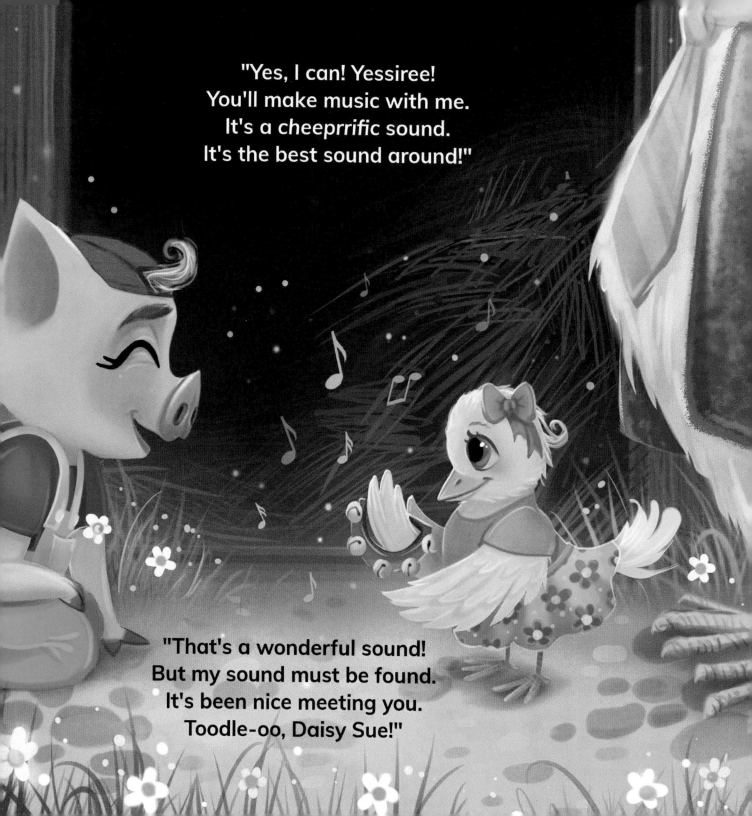

"Yes, I can! Yessiree!
You'll make music with me.
It's a *cheeprrific* sound.
It's the best sound around!"

"That's a wonderful sound!
But my sound must be found.
It's been nice meeting you.
Toodle-oo, Daisy Sue!"

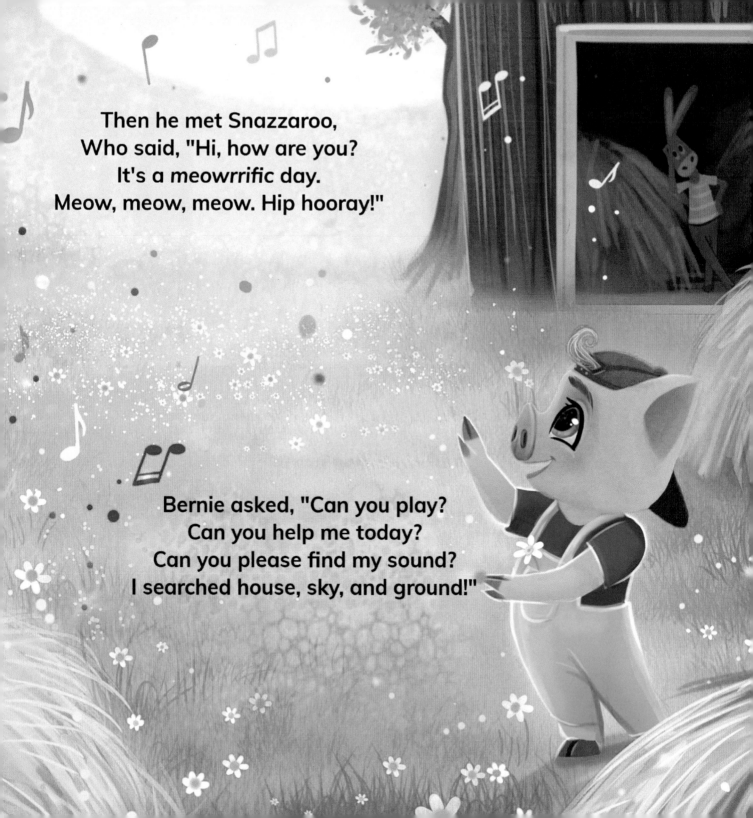

Then he met Snazzaroo,
Who said, "Hi, how are you?
It's a *meowrrific* day.
Meow, meow, meow. Hip hooray!"

Bernie asked, "Can you play?
Can you help me today?
Can you please find my sound?
I searched house, sky, and ground!"

Then he met Hunteroo,
Who said, "Hi, how are you?
It's a *bowrrific* day.
Bow, wow, wow. Hip hooray!"

Bernie asked, "Can you play?
Can you help me today?
Can you please find my sound?
I searched house, sky, and ground!"

"Yes, I can! Yessiree!
You'll make music with me.
It's a *bowrrific* sound.
It's the best sound around!"

"That's a wonderful sound!
But my sound must be found.
It's been nice meeting you.
Toodle-oo, Hunteroo!"

Then he met Cuddlycoo,
Who said, "Hi, how are you?
It's a *baarrific* day.
Baa, baa, baa. Hip hooray!"

Bernie asked, "Can you play?
Can you help me today?
Can you please find my sound?
I searched house, sky, and ground!"

"Yes, I can! Yessiree!
You'll make music with me.
It's a *baarrific* sound.
It's the best sound around!"

"That's a wonderful sound!
But my sound must be found.
It's been nice meeting you.
Toodle-oo, Cuddlycoo!"

Then he met Trotteroo,
Who said, "Hi, how are you?
It's a *neighrrific* day.
Neigh, neigh, neigh. Hip hooray!"

Bernie asked, "Can you play?
Can you help me today?
Can you please find my sound?
I searched house, sky, and ground!"

"Yes, I can! Yessiree!
You'll make music with me.
It's a *neighrrific* sound.
It's the best sound around!"

"That's a wonderful sound!
But my sound must be found.
It's been nice meeting you.
Toodle-oo, Trotteroo!"

Then he met Moozeedoo,
Who said, "Hi, how are you?
It's a *moorrific* day.
Moo, moo, moo. Hip hooray!"

Bernie asked, "Can you play?
Can you help me today?
Can you please find my sound?
I searched house, sky, and ground!"

Then he met Quackeroo,
Who said, "Hi, how are you?
It's a quackrrific day.
Quack, quack, quack. Hip hooray!"

Bernie asked, "Can you play?
Can you help me today?
Can you please find my sound?
I searched house, sky, and ground!"

Then he met Doodledoo,
Who said, "Hi, how are you?
It's a *heerrific* day.
Hee, haw, haw. Hip hooray!"

Bernie asked, "Can you play?
Can you help me today?
Can you please find my sound?
I searched house, sky, and ground!"

"Yes, I can! Yessiree!
You'll make music with me.
It's a *heerrific* sound.
It's the best sound around!"

"That's a wonderful sound!
But my sound must be found.
It's been nice meeting you.
Toodle-oo, Doodledoo!"

With an *oinkity* sigh,
Bernie said, "Me, oh my!
All my friends have a sound,
But my sound wasn't found!
Oh, no! What should I do?
I feel *oinkity* blue."

Bernie thought of this day,
When he heard piggies say,
"Go away! Do not stay.
Leave our house made of hay."

So, he rested out there,
Sitting on his stump chair.
Bernie heard what to do.
Mama's words were so true.

"You must start with your heart.
That's the best place to start.
It's the oinkity, oinkity,
Best place to start!"

Now he knew what to do.
He was not feeling blue.
He was not feeling bad.
He was *oinkity* glad!

He was *oinkity, oinkity,
Oinkity* glad!

Bernie laughed and he rapped.
And he tappity tapped!
Bernie danced and he clapped.
And he snappity snapped!

Bernie sat down out there,
Working on his stump chair.
He had help from a hare.
Not a sound could compare!

Bernie's song was now done.
It was oinkity fun!
It was oinkity, oinkity,
Oinkity fun!

Bernie walked home that day
To his house made of hay.
Saying, "Oink, oink! Hooray!
It's an oinkrrific day!
It's an oinkity, oinkity,
oinkrrific day!"

All the piggies said, "Yay!
You are back home to stay!
We were not nice to you,
And our words were not true.

"We are sorry and sad.
We were oinkity bad!
We were oinkity, oinkity,
Oinkity bad!"

Mama stood very near,
Saying, "Let me be clear.
They were mad. They were sad.
Now they're *oinkity* glad.

"We are *all* proud of you.
And your *pigphony* too!
Show us now from your heart.
It's the best place to start.

"It's the *oinkity, oinkity,*
Best place to start!"

Bernie laughed and he rapped.
And he tappity tapped!
And he danced, and he clapped.
And he snappity snapped!

Every friend came around
And they joined in the sound.
Every oink, quack, and caw,
Every moo, cheep, and baa!

Every neigh and meow,
Every cluck and bow wow.
Bernie said, "Hip hooray!
It's an oinkrrific day!

It's an oinkity, oinkity,
Oinkrrific day!"

If you feel sad and blue,
There's a sound just for you.
It is kind. It is real.
It's the love that you feel.

Now you know what to do.
Trust the words that ring true.
Find the love in your heart.
That's the best place to start.

It's the oinkity, oinkity,
Best place to start!

A Note to the Reader
Tips for Parents and Teachers

Thank you for purchasing *An Oinkrrific Day!* This poem-story teaches self-confidence, kindness, and forgiveness while introducing classroom musical instruments and barnyard animal sounds. Here are a few tips:

1. Ask the children, "How many piggies are in Bernie's family? Count each piggy. Can you name each of the brothers and sisters?"

2. Mama pig tells Bernie to listen to his heart. This means to do what makes him happy. Encourage children to tell you what makes them happy.

3. Each barnyard animal makes a unique sound (for example, "Moo, moo, moo!"). Encourage children to guess the animal before turning the page.

4. Every animal Bernie meets plays a musical instrument. Help children strum, shake, tap, pat, or play imaginary instruments (see the next page).

For TWENTY fun activities, download *Oinkrrific Activities for Parents and Teachers* at www.jeanvoicedart.com.

If you enjoyed the book, please post
a positive review on Amazon.com.

Thank you!

Jean

Bernie's barnyard buddies each played
a different musical instrument.

 xylophone

 triangle

 tambourine

 harmonica

 wrist bells

 cowbell

 maracas

 claves

 ukulele

 drum

Which animal played each instrument?
Which is your favorite?

Go to www.jeanvoicedart.com
to download FREE educational giveaways.

Here is a little peek at Bernie's rap.
You can write a rap too! What will you write?

An Oinkrrific Pigphony

It's Bernie the pig
From a house made of hay.
Please listen to these words
I'm speaking today.

It really doesn't matter
What others say to you.
Listen to your heart
For words that are true.

It's oinkity FUN and FREE!
Download ALL three pages.

www.jeanvoicedart.com

About Jean Voice Dart

Growing up next to the Illinois cornfields, Jean listened to chirping crickets, chased lightning bugs, and created imaginative stories, songs, and poems. As a teenager, she wrote *The Pig Who Found Music*, a heart-warming story about little Bernie, later entitled, *An Oinkrrific Day!*

Multiple life challenges empowered Jean to become a passionate music therapist, teacher, creative arts and performing arts coach, and author. She created the *Bully-Busting Adventures* series to help children, youth, and adults reset their self-esteem, boost their joy and confidence, and share their unique gifts with the world.

Jean currently lives in California with her husband, Matt, their dachshund, Rudy, tabby cat, Rami, and several families of birds and squirrels.

About Anastasia Yatsunenko

Anastasia Yatsunenko was born and raised in Ukraine. She graduated from Kyiv University as a designer-illustrator and now works in the city, taking time to relax and observe nature and animals.

Spending time with her grandfather is something very dear to Anastasia's heart. She especially enjoys seeing the cows, horses, rabbits, chickens, and pigs, and watching the swans and ducks in the village lake.

Today Anastasia and Jean are delighted to have found one another and join together to create the *Bully-Busting Adventures* series books, including the partner book, *An Oinkrrific Day! Activity and Coloring Book.*

An Oinkrrific Day!

Activity and Coloring Book

By Jean Voice Dart

Illustrated by Anastasia Yatsunenko

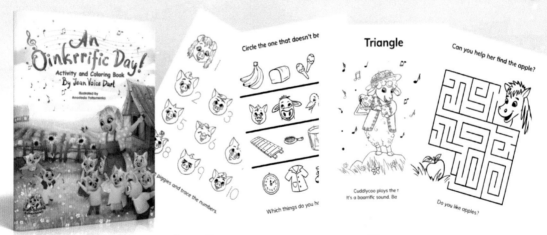

Ready for some smiles?
Try these FIFTY creative and FUN activities!

Yippee!

Looking for more?
Get FREE Oinkrrific Giveaways!

Download these FOUR FREE, FUN, educational giveaways as my gift to YOU!

* Two coloring and activity worksheets
* Complete lyrics to Bernie's "Oinkrrific Pigphony"
* "Oinkrrific Activities for Parents and Teachers" (for home and school)

Go to www.jeanvoicedart.com for your free download.

Made in the USA
Coppell, TX
22 June 2021